Echo Heights

Pat McDonald

Copyright © 2024 Pat McDonald. All rights reserved.

No part of this book may be reproduced or transmitted in any form or by any means, graphic, electronic, or mechanical, including photocopying, recording, taping, or by any information storage retrieval system, without the permission, in writing, of the publisher. For more information, send an email to support@sbpra.net, Attention: Subsidiary Rights.

Strategic Book Publishing
www.sbpra.net

For information about special discounts for bulk purchases, please contact Strategic Book Publishing, Special Sales, at bookorder@sbpra.net.

ISBN: 978-1-68235-972-3

Dedicated to

*All the Lizzie's who forfeited their lives
and their babies*

Acknowledgements:

Whilst this is a work of fiction, some elements of this story occurred during the time the author worked as a manager within a large Victorian Asylum; I leave it to the individual reader to determine which. However, none of the characters contained here are real, any resemblance to anyone alive or dead, is unintentional.

PROLOGUE

My name is Winston Henry. The only reason I mention this is 'cos in my family line names were really important and as far as I remember my daddy telling me about our family ancestors, it wasn't always the case we got last names. Of course, I'm going way back in my Jamaican family tree when most people were known only by their first name. In our case, Henry was a distant grand pappy if I'm to believe what my daddy told me, this was how we got the last name of Henry. It was dedicated to him when the first of our line was baptised into Christian ways and they chose the name so we would remember where we came from.

I've never been to Jamaica, even though I always wanted to go. We had no money for paying the boat fare. In those days travelling by aeroplane wasn't the done thing like it is now. As to me, I was born here, so I am a Britisher. My daddy came over in the 50s when a lot of immigrants were brought in after the big war to help the country get back on its feet. They needed more workers after a lot of men (and women) died fighting. My folk came because they thought we could prosper better here, like the streets were paved with gold – that sort of thing.

They weren't of course – paved with gold I mean. I doubt whether any of my folk ever saw real gold, most of the wedding rings I ever saw 'mongst our kind were too dark to be anything other than brass – you know those rings they used to hang up curtains years ago. A new start for them I reckon meant more of the same hard work in a country that was cold most of the time. You hear stories 'bout how Jamaica is all parties or lazing around in the sunshine, but then a hot climate can be very tiring. It didn't much matter, my daddy told me, if you didn't have a bed to sleep in, you just slept on the beach where it was warm. I think he was only reminiscing when the weather got really cold here. O'course, I didn't know any different. The idea of sunshine and lazing appealed to me back then.

I wasn't surprised my folks eventually went back to live in Jamaica because they did nothing but moan about this country. I never asked how they got the money to get there. They said they had kin folk who would put them up till they could find work and somewhere to live. At first I had dreams I'd go to join them, but you get into working and surviving. I wasn't really much into partying or a lazy life by then. Anyway, it wasn't too long 'afore poor health first took my mammy and right after my daddy joined her. I didn't really know any of my kin to consider going to Jamaica to live after that.

I survived going through my schooling days, a single black kid in a class of thirty but the novelty for the others soon wore off. I won't say they resented me, 'cos I don't think that's why I was bullied by some of them back then, more not knowing about black people. Maybe even a bit of resentment, us black folk having more of a sense of community 'mongst our own. We was church going, most of the other kids' families weren't then. Our kind was 'god fearing' which for us kids meant discipline, respecting yer elders or else God would punish us.

As a little kid I was a'feared of God most of the time. I felt mighty weak. So being labelled 'god fearing' as I grew up didn't encourage me to be much in favour of church stuff. I got to be more a'feared of the folk who were though. I 'spose it was why I kept to myself when I was at school, my way of avoiding other kids who wanted to get me into trouble back then.

The actual learning at school I saw as a way of getting a better life. So I studied my books which meant I didn't mix well with the others who didn't want to. They ridiculed me 'cos I did. I've done okay though. I got into nursing which I think was a first for my family. It suited me alright. I'm not what you call a sociable person anyway so when I made a move up to working in the old Asylum I reckon I found where I wanted to be. I've been there a lot of years now. Even though the Asylum is a depressing place, I can honestly say I don't let it get me down. The patients are mostly like me, they don't talk much, medication sees to that. As does fear of saying stuff to the doctors, because everything they say is used as evidence of one mental illness or another isn't it? If they smile too much it's taken as 'inappropriate' smiling, whilst not smiling at all is considered a depressive state; they can't win.

So that's all really, my name is Winston Henry and I work up at the Asylum.

1

How I came to work at Echo Heights, that's what they called the Asylum in those days, I think to make the place seem less depressing, was because there always seemed to be vacancies there. It's not the kind of place you ever considered progressive, well not a place to go if you got ambitions to get promoted. Mental illness nursing didn't open up any opportunities back then, so most ambitious nurses avoided it like the plague. For me it was more about the type of patients I would get, like I said I'm not a very sociable sort of person. I heard the place contained people who had been there for years, what you called 'institutionalised' and wouldn't be inclined to be sociable either. I wanted an easy life and to avoid unnecessary mixing.

Yes, there were a lot of patients who were there for most of their lives and many of them died there. Echo Heights had a chapel and even a graveyard tucked away out of plain sight. The Asylum wasn't built as a place where people went to get 'cured'. If you read stuff going a long way back, what treatments they used were really harsh and experimental, so you never got to hear about anyone leaving cured of what they were admitted with.

No, it was more a place of containment, somewhere to put the craziest of people out of the way of normal society. Institutionalisation in old times meant breaking of the spirit of those most tormented, so in one sense they just fizzled out like a candle's brightness might before it goes out completely. Of course, I wasn't there then and a lot changed when they invented psychotropic drugs like antidepressants, antianxiety medications, antipsychotics, even stimulants making it possible for 'short stay' patients to get admitted to be 'cured' then released.

Even before I went to work there I got to hear how strange the place was. There was always one colourful story or another doing the rounds. Yes, a lot of people thought I must be crazy myself to want to work there. Those were people who believed the stories they heard about the place. I never did because they were all second hand, you know, like Chinese Whispers, they got bits added on so you couldn't trust much of what you heard.

The truth was I never saw anything out of the ordinary all the years I worked the day shift up at Echo Heights. Any slight movement, you know, out of the corner of the eye on my peripheral vision, was explainable one way or another. There was always plenty of long stay patients around acting out, doing all kinds of crazy stuff to account for . . . well just about everything I saw really. Sometimes the day shift was so manic I'd have settled for a manifestation floating harmlessly around a bend in a corridor, none of which registered more than at a subliminal level, so I didn't dwell on those. I much prefer peace, it must be in my genes.

I always envied the night shift in those days. I figured they got an easier life because every one of the 'crazies' were fast asleep and well medicated. At the most hectic of my daytime shifts I even let my envy spill over into anger. I wanted so much to get a piece of the action, or rather the inaction. Maybe there really was something in my genes, with a streak of the Jamaican laziness my daddy always talked about. What I saw was the night staff getting paid to take naps in between doing the old 'bed state' patrol of the hospital they did at around midnight, there was very little in the way of paperwork for them to do.

I saw their reports (if you could call them that) in the ward register which was a routine repetitive one liner you didn't need much imagination or skill to record. Hell, even a child could write 'fast asleep all night' which in itself wasn't proof of any routine inspection of the patients. The day staff got them comatose ready for the night shift, didn't they?

My enquiries of management to get transferred to night duty were always met with the same reply of, '*there are no vacancies at the present time*', which eventually led me to abandon my attempts for a transfer. The way I saw it there must have been some kind of nepotism going on so I wouldn't stand a chance. I didn't think there was prejudice because I knew from other folk there was a variety of different racial backgrounds amongst those who worked nights around the hospital.

In my more sympathetic moments, I let myself believe the personal circumstances of night rota staff might have been reason enough for them working on nights and maybe management were being sympathetic in considering them. You know, like out of necessity because of needing child cover and they couldn't afford to get paid help, so had to rely on their partners who worked in the day time to cover the nights whilst they worked. That's not much of a life if you never saw each other though, is it? In my early days we didn't get paid much, least ways not to be able to keep a family on.

I don't have that problem. I've got no family you see. In my case I live alone. I like it that way. Well so I tell myself anyway especially when I hear how others live. I'm not much for mixing socially which is why I know I would suit the night shift, not everybody likes their own company like me. We have a few of those sociable sorts on days, you know, always wanting to talk, telling you all about their problems, they just never shut up. I keep myself to myself and wouldn't dream 'bout telling anyone anything personal. My business is my own, nobody else's. I have no inclination to share myself with anyone.

The divorced ones are the worst. You get chapter and verse about the breakdown of their relationships. Lord, how I hate having to listen to the whole sorry split, blow by blow account, they drive me crazy. I could even end up one of the inpatients. I try to take my breaks alone and even if I don't go to the staff room they follow me to the canteen where they invade my table when I'm trying to read the paper or a book. I go to great lengths to move any spare chair away from where I sit, to another table, but that don't stop them finding one and joining me. I never understood why, it's not like I encourage them.

I 'spose it's because they think I'm a good listener when, in fact, I just don't want to talk about myself, so they take advantage. I don't go to the canteen very often anyway. Even with the subsidies on the meals I wouldn't eat there every day. I bring a bit of food from home when it's nice weather to go outside to find a quiet place, like the bowling green, hoping I'll get left in peace to eat it.

You get one or two of the patients come out and sit down next to you. I don't have much time for chatting with them either, it's hard work sometimes and not like getting a break from them is it? Mostly though the old timers just come up to me wanting a light for a cigarette nub they've found thrown on the ground somewhere, so I carry a box of matches on me at all times. I don't smoke myself, so when they're asking for a cigarette I can't oblige or more likely they just want a light, after which they go away.

They aren't like the staff, they don't want to tell you all about themselves. Why would they when the psychiatrists ask them to do that all the time, so they probably get fed up of talking anyway. They're more like me just wanting to sit quietly, feel the sun on their face out in the fresh air away from the depressing atmosphere they live in inside the place with the stench a lot of folk living together can make. I can appreciate this after all I'm in the same boat as them aren't I? Except I get to go home at the end of the day, even if it's basic as homes go. No I'm not one for mixing or chatting.

Mind you the doctors are a strange lot anyway. I was doing a ward round the other day with one of the consultants. It's different for psychiatrics to general medicine, the patients aren't in bed all day like them. No, you sit in a consulting room with a whole bunch of other people where your patient (one allocated to you for their care) is brought in for their assessment session with the doctor. First though, you update the doctor about your patient, things like why they were admitted, what their symptoms are, whether they have been sectioned (under the Mental Health Act) or are voluntary, that sort of thing. If they have been sectioned then it's making an assessment of whether they are a danger to themselves or to anyone else. Afterwards you fetch them in.

It must be quite frightening to the patient having so many people present like doctors, nurses and other professionals. We even have student doctors, being a teaching hospital, so they come here for the experience. Ward rounds can get mob-handed right enough. I can see for the patient it must be quite scary, you can see by their faces. I often think the whole set up isn't helpful to getting better. There's something a bit strange about taking someone who is disturbed out of the real world because they aren't able to cope with it, putting them in this truly depressing place to get them fit to go back into the real world, must be confusing to a lot of them.

The longer they stay the more difficult they must find surviving back in the world outside. You can see by the number of times they get readmitted. At least inside the asylum they are accepted for who they are, outside there is little understanding of mental illness problems so they aren't readily accepted. They get quite isolated and shunned by others. I can understand how they must feel from when I was the token black child in a classroom full of white kids.

Anyway, on this particular day I've been given this woman who was really crazy. She'd been admitted because she said she was raped by the devil in broad daylight as she was walking down the street. She insists she's been really scared ever since she joined a witch's coven where she works at a factory somewhere in town. Yes, of course I felt sorry for her, she did look terrified because she said she knew the Devil could find her even in here. I thought 'psychotic' immediately and she was in need of some drugs to quieten her down, only the consultant asked the medical students what they thought after they took her back out to the ward. They of course thought the same as me.

It surprised me when the consultant said the first thing we needed to do was find out whether there *was* a witch's coven where she worked! The medical students looked as amazed as I felt. I think sometimes, maybe the doctors have worked closed in here for too long, they often seem as crazy, if not crazier, than the patients. Rumour has it there was one of the old doctors who used to keep a gun in his desk draw claiming the 'lions' were roaring in the common room. I don't know how true the story is, he's not around now. I think if doctors can eventually lose it altogether the same could happen to anyone working here, which was another reason why I kept myself to myself as much as possible.

I guess this was why they got rid of the doctor's house at the top end of the hospital. Years ago the Asylum doctor lived there on the premises, so he never got to go home *outside* like we do. It's hard sometimes keeping an eye on reality after all, like I said, 'asylum' is about taking people away from 'reality' to be put into a place where they can feel safe, although not for the poor woman who saw the Devil everywhere, she didn't feel safe at all.

How free from reality could you make living together with a whole lot of strange people? Well that's got to be very unreal, however much you tried to build a 'community', there was never going to be a time when you managed a calm balanced atmosphere. There was always a new one just coming in needing calming down with a few pills. The other treatments could be worse. Some of the older staff have stories to tell of those and although not wanting to hear them, there was always someone who seemed too keen to tell you or maybe even secretly missed it. That's what I mean about how working in an Asylum can get to you, we were just as shut inside as the patients even though we got out every day we couldn't escape from the place altogether.

2

No, I never saw anything untoward when I worked the day shift, although I felt things I couldn't explain or was told about what other people claimed they saw. Where I worked was up at the top, on the third floor, in an old sprawling institution called Echo Heights, the general intake ward for acute admissions. The ward was run by the consultant with the strange question about witch's covens. He supported the idea of 'community treatment' where everyone helped each other. It's much like 'One flew over the cuckoo's nest', you know that film with Jack Nicolson where everyone sat around in a circle (medical staff interspersed with all the patients) waiting for someone to say something.

You knew it was going to be the newest patient who did because they are the craziest or aren't used to being there, so when the silence gets too much for them they have to start talking about how they feel. It's generally some paranoid rambling about who's out to get them. Whether it's Satan or someone else, they let rip until another patient chips in to accuse them of talking about them, then all hell breaks loose with a few of the more sedated ones getting upset and start to cry.

I know I sound disrespectful when I say they are 'crazy', but that was why they were admitted right? Over the years I must have met several Jesus Christs as well as a whole range of famous people or those laying claim to being related to someone famous. You know you're going to get a lot of friction when you have two people who think they are Jesus admitted at the same time; it's an explosion waiting to happen.

Echo Heights

I never did understand how this was meant to be therapeutic making them mingle together with other distressed people. I used to think it was so unlike the real world outside. Well until they closed all the mental hospitals and put them back in the community where an over concentration of sick ex-inpatients created the same dysfunctional world outside. Of course, without the asylums anyone getting sick has nowhere to go, so they have to stay at home if they have a home that is. They call it 'community treatment' the same as the Consultant did on my ward, now using teams of people visiting them at home. Personally I reckon there is precious little of it going on. Stands to reason, there are too many people for the small teams to visit and they are so widespread and move around a lot, only visiting when there's an emergency situation.

Some smaller (and seedier) hotels saw a gap in the market and a way of making money being used for housing the mentally ill. A lot of old patients, and new, ended up on the streets because they didn't know how to look after themselves. They were never going to get a job to be able to afford somewhere to live. As time goes by, the world accepts this as the status quo doesn't it? Only now it's a collection of poor souls living in a world which is generally unsafe for everyone.

In a community treatment meeting I always felt like I was there as a 'bouncer' to control any violent fights that broke out. I suppose because of how I'm built, being six foot and solid made like. I try to keep myself in shape, unlike some of the other staff. You would never have believed how violent two people claiming to be Jesus can be, I should know because I had to break them up. It was more than just an "I am Spartacus" moment!

Anyway, this wasn't how I saw the job of a male nurse, yet it was expected of me being stronger than the women. They must have thought I could take the odd black eye or swollen lip during the kafuffle. I never saw any of the doctors step up though and a weedier lot you never did see. When things got really violent they would leg it as fast as they could leaving us nurses to sort the patients out.

Usually, a really bad upset would need a couple of days to get things back on an even keel. Community treatment I thought was meant to cut down on the use of drugs to control violent patients yet we were forced to use more to keep control after these outbursts.

No, I reckon 'community treatment' has its downside. I wouldn't like to defend its application against all the other treatments on offer. I know it was meant to be progressive in the day, an alternative therapy to sticking a needle in their arm, pumping them full of Largactil or Chlorpromazine. The really depressed or the catatonic ones would get ECT, that's electroconvulsive therapy, to shock them out of their withdrawn state. I can't say it was a pleasant thing to watch them being given an electric current through their bodies, even if it did work in a lot of cases, about 70-90% they reckon. One of the side effects could be loss of memory which returned sometime later in most of the cases, even though there was talk of the possibility of some brain damage. They rated it in extreme cases of depression and brought a lot of people back from an inert state.

Anyway, I digress, as I was talking about strange things I've felt I couldn't explain. It was after one of these community meetings when I had to rush to the toilet. The lavatories were in an area we used as a spill over for the patient records. The room had those old wooden racks either side of a central walkway containing hundreds of patient's notes collected over the years and filed on them, the lavatory being at the bottom end. Space was at a premium in those days because patient's notes were all hard copy files, being before we got computers.

I rushed quickly straight down the middle of the filing room being in a bit of a hurry (it had been a long session requiring a lot of bladder control) and I walked straight through a patch of very cold resistant air. It felt like one of those moments you see in movies where they show someone walking through the body of a ghost. In my case there was nothing to see, it just felt - well cold and a bit resistant, like I imagine it would pushing through blancmange, is only how I can describe it. I neither stopped nor pondered much, being in a bit of a hurry to get to the urinals. The only thing I remember is, given the urgency of my need to pee, it took me a long time before I was able to pass water! The other thing was it didn't happen on the way back, thankfully, so I put the whole thing down to my urgent need, which is probably why I completely forgot about it until the priest came, which I'll get to.

This is the first time I've recalled this day for a long time, I certainly didn't mention anything to anyone else at the time. Not that I ever saw anything like other people claimed they did, must have been because I took what people told me with a pinch of salt. There was always someone with a story to tell. I just assumed they made them up to get attention and like I said I avoided people as far as I could most of the time.

It wasn't just colleagues on my ward though. One time I was queuing for something to eat in the canteen, when one of the staff from the semi-secure unit on the second floor just below our ward, was behind me in the queue and suddenly asked me what we were up to the night before. I must have looked pretty blank – well I wasn't night shift was I? He said whatever was going on with all the banging around we must have been moving furniture. I just shrugged thinking maybe they had an incident on the ward. Only the floors are really thick in these old Asylums, none of your tacky workmanship like on today's buildings, they were built to last. My mental asylum, Echo Heights, was built in the 1880's and might not be the oldest one, but that's a hell of a long time to last, isn't it?

When I got back on the ward I was curious enough about the comment made I did check the ward records for the previous night finding nothing recorded, just the usual *'slept well'*, *'everything quiet'*. When I mentioned his comment to someone they just shrugged pointing to the mirror in the ward office like it must have been when the mirror slipped off the wall. Later I heard two people whispering to each other. They were laughing because at the time our ward cleaner, a small Afro-Caribbean woman, who I thought strange, because she wore a huge wooden cross six or seven inches long and about an inch thick, on a leather cord around her neck, found the mirror outside the office propped up against the corridor wall.

I don't know this woman, her name I think is Joyce, who everyone makes fun of because she told stories about having to clean around a male nurse who would stand watching her, which everyone seemed to believe. Not knowing who the night staff were I couldn't really imagine anyone doing that. I always thought of them as sitting in the office with their feet up, in which case she could have hoovered the floor without any obstruction. Mostly she came in to clean at the changeover of the day staff with night staff when they were going through 'handover' so I can't see how there could be someone standing in her way.

The way some of them told the story though was embellished with a description the male nurse wore a really old style uniform like they did in the 1930s. Some people thought it hugely amusing Joyce believed her wooden cross would protect her – hell I have suffered enough black eyes and cut lips to know it wouldn't. Some patients pack a hefty punch. A wooden cross, however big, wasn't going to stop one of our patients if they went on the rampage, they aren't vampires. Well maybe one or two thought they were.

Most of the stuff I heard about the night shift I thought was a ploy to protect the staff who worked it. You heard how they discouraged other nurses from applying to do nights. I thought because it must be such a cushy number they wanted to keep them all to themselves. They weren't ever going to have to sit through a 'community treatment' therapy meeting or have to break up a fight like me because that stuff never happened at night. Most of the patients were given medication anyway, so I reckon they were guaranteed a peaceful night shift.

There was a rumour going round the new breed of managers were considering creating a rota system to cover three shifts, mornings, afternoons and nights, by rotating all three in turn to produce what they called a 'shift pattern.' It must have got a heavy knock back from the medical staff, doctors especially didn't want to get involved. I know for certain they liked just working days with the weekends off on call if anything urgent came in, so why would they endorse it? It didn't happen anyway. I just carried on as before, only on the most troublesome of days ever dreamt about getting on the night shift.

3

Some days I wasn't much good at avoiding other staff. I would get cornered by someone wanting a chat or just to talk to someone, usually talk *at* someone. One time during a nice patch of weather I was sitting on a wall in the gardens, next to a large green manicured lawn situated below, out of sight of the main building, where I was able to forget about the drab old asylum which really was as depressing inside as it looked on the outside.

This spot in the old days used to be where they grew vegetables for the hospital kitchen and where the Asylum inmates worked. If you look in the old inpatient ledgers some of them got 'works well in the gardens' as their annual medical assessment! In those days you got the one entry for a whole year's confinement. Now the garden is given over to this bowling green and a lot of flower beds and shrubbery.

This is a flat, well cared for lawn I noticed occasionally had a bit of 'fairy ring' giving dry patches to spoil the very lush surface. Not you understand I know much about these things or even gardening, I don't have one of my own because I live in a flat. I did once spot someone here prodding holes in it with a garden fork before putting some kind of fertiliser down. I don't think the bowling green has ever been used by any of the inmates since they laid the turf. I hear mostly it's used by the staff sports club and visitors for playing matches. I never have seen anyone playing bowls though and I've worked all sorts of days on my shift even weekends.

Anyway, on this one fine day, I'm sitting on a low wall at the side of the green, eating my lunch. I brought some left over Jerk chicken from home. I still make it myself from my mammy's own recipe and she really knew how to cook proper Jamaican food. I'm sitting taking in the warmth from the sun with a slight breeze on my face, just enjoying the break. With my eyes closed I feel a draught of air as someone sits down next to me. I reach into my pocket for the matches I keep there whilst stifling my inevitable sigh at being disturbed. When I open my eyes I see the face of our ward receptionist, a thirty something woman whose name escaped me at that moment. This was a newish idea for psychiatric wards to be run by non-medical people, the idea being it freed us nurses up from doing admin so we could concentrate on patient care.

She tried to smile at me but failed miserably. For a moment I feel trapped into yet another round of someone's personal relationship problems. Turned out I was way off the mark, her concerns being ones of a more 'unworldly' kind. The story she told me stopped me eating my chicken. It wasn't so much *what* she said, more the fear I can see in her face, her whole body was trembling so much her voice quivered as she spoke. I could tell she was trying to hold herself together, to look calm.

She made no mention of why she was telling *me*. We have barely exchanged a few words since she was appointed and to be honest up till this conversation I thought here was someone like me who keeps her own council. I was even quite attracted to her because I admire her for her reserve. The thing is I steer clear of any romantic entanglements because of a previous relationship I had with a woman who turned out to be way too verbal and dramatic for me to be living with.

Yes, it was a mistake, one I should have been well prepared to avoid, having lived with my Jamaican parents who seemed only to be able to shout at each other which I found extremely tiring. I imagined them going back to Jamaica where the heat somehow made them wind down then fizzled out from the sheer exhaustion of living together. Anyways, I digress. Here *was* the only woman I came close to admiring since that one mistake all those years ago, and she sought me out to confide in me!

It occurred, she told me, after the day staff left for the evening, only she was so engrossed in the completion of the weekly ward stationery order which she hadn't finished, she missed them leaving. First of all she popped home, living as she does across the road from the asylum, to make sure her dogs were okay before she came back in to finish the task.

Every one of the day shift must have gone home and there was no sign of the night shift, they were probably doing something around the hospital. She immediately got on with her order which needed to be in that day before she could finally go home for the night.

Just outside her office door there's an area with a sink where all us staff make ourselves drinks. There's a window, one of the old sash ones overlooked when they did some minor refurbishment. This window hadn't been part of any of the Health and Safety inspections or highlighted as needing to be replaced, because there isn't a fire escape outside. Therefore, they left it alone. Most of us thought it was responsible for the arctic blasts we suffered throughout the ward during very bad weather. When it was really windy weather it would rattle loudly being so loosely fitted.

With the door closed for extra quiet she suddenly heard a loud banging as if someone was standing outside the window pounding on it with their fists. The way she said, "We're three floors up" was so packed with fear, it sent a chill down my spine. As for her, she was trembling with the recollection of it. Eventually, she plucked up the courage to open the door to go out there and found no one there. Still shaking she turned back into the room pulling the door closed behind her, to find a male nurse standing quite still staring at her.

For a moment she told me she was riveted to the spot, then managed to walk around him to sit back at the desk where her telephone was, thinking about calling for help although not knowing who she could call. He seemed to follow her passage with his eyes as if *he could see her, then just walked away disappearing through the door which she was sure she closed behind her on the way back in.*

She stopped talking, waiting for some reaction from me. I admit being lost for words. In fact, so shocked I couldn't give her the reply she obviously sought. She then told me she hadn't seen the nurse around the hospital before, but was wearing one of the old style uniforms, the ones you can see in the framed photographs displayed on the walls up at the top end of the hospital in the new elaborately refurbished main entrance to the hospital. The way she stared fixedly at me for a response chilled me momentarily. How could I answer her?

The similarities between this story and the one doing the rounds told by Joyce the cleaner was almost identical, apart from the pounding on the window bit. My natural scepticism about the whole ghost thing made me consider this could be some kind of joint hysteria. After all the imagination is a curious thing apt to catch people whilst they are anxious or stressed in some way.

She was by her own admission fraught over missing getting the ward stationery order done, not wanting to miss the week's deadline which meant we would as sure as not run out of some of the most important statutory forms we would certainly need to use the following week if we got a new acute admission. Like I said we didn't have computers in them days.

The longer the silence between us went on, the more difficulty I had formulating an appropriate response. The truth was I really had no idea what to tell her or even how to comfort her obvious distress. I could hardly tell her to pull herself together or not to be so silly. I think she would have been offended by it. To show any idea I might believe her, well I just couldn't because at the time I really didn't believe her, so to have agreed with her would have left me open to ridicule by the same people who were already laughing at Joyce the cleaner. I much preferred not to attract any attention. All I wanted was an easy life.

What I did say I admit was a bit of a lame suggestion, that perhaps she should mention what happened to the ward doctor to see what he thought. By the way she suddenly stood up and silently studied my face before she walked away, left me in no doubt about her disappointment in me. I don't know why she chose me to confide in or, in fact, if I was the only one she tried to talk to, all I know is she never mentioned the incident again and no one else raised it with me.

Afterwards, I noticed an air of coolness towards me whenever we were alone in the office which crushed any stray idea I might have got about asking her out for a drink sometime. I guess that boat sailed after because we never really talked much other than about a patient or some other work related matter. I certainly didn't tell anyone about it, mostly because I rarely spoke to anyone other than about the patients in my care.

From the rare conversations I had with other members of staff, I tried as much as possible to avoid anyone's personal life. From what I did hear, I led quite a charmed life compared to most of theirs. I put this down to being single. I got none of the issues they saw fit to tell me about on those occasions when I couldn't avoid them. Whether they told me about their actual divorce drama or the number of squabbles they were having, there didn't seem to be many of the staff, if any at all, who could be in happy relationships. If anything all this put me off any kind of personal relationship if all they ever did was make people unhappy.

Of course I also had none of their problems with kids I overheard doing the gossip circuit, because I didn't have any children either. I must admit from what I heard about wayward or unruly offspring they all seemed out of control, I was glad I didn't have any. I was yet to hear any claims of well-adjusted children amongst the staff. Somehow that fit in with the overall environment of where they worked and I often wondered if the two went together. I mean, did staff with dysfunctional private lives seek refuge to work here in this

Asylum or did working here make them dysfunctional? You've got to admit the coincidence was great.

I heard one of the nurses got reported to child services by an anonymous neighbour who accused her of child abuse. She was beside herself with astonishment and anger at such an accusation and was now in the process of trying to prove the claim was a malicious one. She knew once you got on the child abuse register it was almost impossible to get the claims wiped off.

Another young nurse, who recently married one of the doctors, after returning home from work one day, some ten days after her wedding, found her clothes and personal things packed waiting for her outside their flat door with the locks changed. I don't suppose hers was the shortest marriage on record but must have come close. This was how the personal tragedies were mounting up leading me to believe proportionally the happenings must surely be excessive, if not abnormal, for one small group of people.

I began to hear the word jinxed being bandied around. Everyone (apart from me) seemed convinced these disasters were something to do with working where we did. I made no enquiries as to whether any of the other wards had similar patterns of personal trauma amongst their staff, mainly because that would mean I would have to talk to them and discuss my ward's personal problems and I steered clear of that sort of thing. As far as I was concerned gossiping was taboo.

4

It was during one of the daily staff ward meetings someone first raised the idea of having an exorcism. I'm not really a religious person, despite my mammy and daddy's Baptist teachings, this seemed a bit extreme to me, although several of the staff were keen to make enquiries. On admission we were obliged to ask patients about their religious beliefs because all religions were covered by either a visiting priest or a vicar depending on their denomination, both covering the Asylum from nearby churches. We kept a daily record of the patients in a list given to the Priest or the Reverend so they could provide the inpatients with 'spiritual' care.

When we told the reverend about the level of anxiety amongst the staff after having seen 'ghostly' activity on the ward, he suggested these people would probably benefit from some counselling and perhaps the hospital could provide it. To be honest he sounded as sceptical as I was back then, which I thought odd for someone who believed in God, a spiritual being in Heaven. I wanted to ask him if he believed in Satan given my patient's presenting symptoms. I didn't ask because that would only draw attention to me.

The priest was much more receptive to the idea, saying when he was newly ordained he lived in a vicarage with a very disruptive poltergeist. He explained they are spirits of departed people who for some reason don't want to pass on to the next world. He didn't elaborate any more because he was clear about making us understand the Catholic church no longer did exorcisms, except in extreme cases, which he also didn't explain. Where they did one, they were undertaken by priests who were qualified in exorcism. He wasn't qualified to undertake such a thing. He did say he was happy to come along to bless our ward which might give the staff some relief. He seemed certain he could help. I was surprised he had no curiosity about whether any of us belonged to his church or even if we believed in God. I suppose he did, which was all that mattered.

If I was to highlight a time when my doubts began to be challenged I would have to say the day the priest first came to bless the ward, although he was to repeat the blessing again at a later time. My own curiosity I suppose drove me to want to witness what he did as much as to see the reaction by the staff to his actions. Not everyone cared to get involved, only a few people like the receptionist Janice (I learnt her name much later) did with one or two of the nurses tagging along. I joined in, very much the voyeur of the group, which the others didn't challenge or call me out as a non-believer, even though they must have known or suspected as I made no secret of it.

The priest arrived ready dressed in his cassock bringing his chasuble which he wore on top. He took out of a small black case he was carrying a neatly folded long priest's stole, which he blessed and kissed before he placed it around his neck letting it hang equally down each side. I later learnt this symbolised the bonds with which Jesus was bound during his Passion and is commonly known to denote the duty to spread the Word of God.

From the same black case he produced a long silver tube-like object which he shook periodically saying, "In the name of the Father and the Son and the Holy Spirit", at various points as we moved around the ward. We attracted curious stares as we progressed, with a little suspicion from some of the more aware patients. I don't think we had any Jesus Christs on the ward thankfully! We followed in his wake as he moved from place to place reciting I know not what. I assumed his words were some kind of prayer or mantra in Latin.

He chose those places of specific areas of spirit activity the others indicated to him, like the receptionist's office where she saw her apparition and the place where Joyce the cleaner cleaned around her male nurse. When he asked if there was anywhere else we wanted him to go I offered the place where I experienced my cold resistant air in the filing room across the corridor which led to the toilets, where the patient records are kept. I didn't explain to them why though. I did get a few curious looks from the others but kept my reasons to myself.

On returning once again across the corridor the priest stopped as if attracted by something at a door asking what was behind it. This was the emergency exit door. The back stairs leading down to ground level which as far as I knew we had never used in all the time I'd worked there. We didn't have a fire escape so this would act as a way out if there was a real fire requiring emergency evacuation. The door at the bottom I knew we kept locked so patients couldn't get out that way. I have no idea where we kept the key. He opened the door, stood quite still at the top of the stairs leading downwards, indicating we might as well cover this, the same as the rest of the ward.

Consequently, we followed him down the stone steps. Half way down, the steps flattened out at a point where there was another closed door off to the side. I can't say I've ever been in this room before or even that its existence ever registered with me, then I don't recall going down this way more than the once to satisfy my curiosity as to where the steps led. When we opened the door, we were hit by some extremely cold air which was strange given there was no window. The room was dark and even switching on a weak overhead naked bulb hanging from the ceiling didn't brighten the room much. We could all see there was nothing in there except to one side there was a wall to wall stone slab at about waist height covering over a half brick wall as if something got sealed in.

I immediately thought of the old style baths I once saw in the pictures of antiquated patient treatments up at the top end of the hospital in what is now a bit of a museum of old pictures and items like straitjackets. I once looked through some of the collection of old books in the library in the old wing next door to the museum which used to be the doctor's house in the old days. Now this room made me shiver with the thought of leaving a patient in here on their own. Other than this odd thought I couldn't think what else the room would have been used for situated where it was off a back staircase; certainly not a store room as it was empty which surprised me given we were short of places to store things. I thought what a wasted opportunity.

I backed out to stand with the others on the flat step outside the room whilst the priest went inside alone. We could hear him begin to deliver his blessing, no doubt shaking the holy water drops around the room, we actually couldn't see him. What I heard above his incantations made my blood freeze! Almost immediately he began his blessing we all heard a deep sonorous sigh as if released from the bowels of hell or some captive presence that was neither the priest nor any one of us standing waiting there. It sent a ripple up my spine making my legs lose all feeling it was so eerie, 'otherworldly' was how I would have said if I had to, although I never have spoken about this to anyone.

Whether the priest heard it I have no idea except he must have as he was standing in the room at the time. He didn't comment when he came back out, he just continued hurriedly down to the bottom of the steps as far as the locked door, whilst we waited where we were, looking into the darkened room, hoping the priest wouldn't take too long to finish his blessing.

When we got back upstairs he made no comment or any assessment of his blessing, he merely disrobed before he left without a word. I can't say I could explain the sound, which was far too loud to be made by the priest, or assess any part of his visit. I can't even say things improved much on the ward after as there was a closing of ranks with no one caring to speak about it or even themselves afterwards, which as far as I was concerned was one positive to come out with a backing off of people wanting to confide in others.

That something occurred during his blessing I have no doubt. What I heard in that room was something being released from somewhere they were trapped, maybe one of those souls the priest told us couldn't pass on after they died. Whether it was or not, I think I became less doubting than I was before and a bit more open minded. That day kind of slipped from my thoughts because shortly after I was asked by management if I still wanted to transfer to the night shift which came out of the blue.

As to eliminating any of the ghosts, well I didn't believe in them at the time so I couldn't comment on anyone else's experiences. I thought the priest could have been directly responsible for my good fortune as I thought I was destined to spend the rest of my working life on the day shift and suddenly here was a change in fortune, or so I thought at the time.

One other possibility crossed my mind, but then I'm a born cynic. I thought maybe it was more to do with me being able to break up any potential physical dispute because there had been yet another spat at the very next community meeting requiring me to intervene. Management hinted I seemed a strong sort of chap who was able to handle myself well which I thought was a curious thing to say given I knew patients at night would be well out of it so there would be little need for those kind of skills.

I didn't care one way or the other why they made the decision settling on me as opposed to anyone else, I knew I wasn't the only one with hopes of covering nights. I wasn't even bothered about there suddenly being a vacancy or why one occurred at the time, I was just glad there was one. It was only later I learnt one of the staff on nights committed suicide; as to why was unclear. There was always going to be rumours especially in a place like this. Later on, as time passed, I was to come to think of the old saying you often heard: "Be careful what you wish for, for surely it will come true."

In my case moving to nights opened up a whole new perspective for me on Echo Heights which unfortunately I would never have believed. I was right about one thing though, night staff did spend their time asleep. I now know not so much a perk as a necessity to keep your own sanity – then I'm jumping ahead with my story which won't tell it like it happened.

5

I sometimes think being unwilling to believe in anything 'unworldly' may have helped me to survive. I do have rather a realistic approach to most things, my maxim being 'everything happens for a reason'. There is a physical explanation for most things. Well I used to. Eventually I got to thinking if you have an old building as ancient as this one, stands to reason with the passage through of so many sad disturbed people, the hospital will have soaked up some of what went on inside over the years, like into the fabric of the building, down to its foundations.

People say, don't they, about a place they live in, being a 'happy home' and must have seen some really happy times. If you can feel that, you must be able to feel how bad a place has been. I didn't believe any of this stuff until I changed to nights. Like I said before then I hadn't seen anything on days and this was still the same place I worked in. From my first night shift things began to change. I felt like I'd been asleep all the while I'd worked the days, then suddenly woke up to how it really was inside Echo Heights.

Did I say I stayed working on the acute intake ward? I just came to work at a different time is all. Yet from the first night I walked onto the ward after all the day staff went home, the place even looked different, somehow darker, shabbier and a lot gloomier. Yes, I know at night we have most of the lights off, only the night lights are on and they are dimmer than the ones we use in the day time. That isn't what I mean.

Even given the lack of bright light, from that very first night, I felt like I was being watched. Ever felt like that? So much so, for the first time since I came to work on the ward, I found myself looking around searching the walls and ceilings for hidden cameras, even in places that might conceal them. I admit I took a chair to stand on to unscrew the fire alarm fitment on the ceiling just to satisfy myself there wasn't anything hidden inside. Crazy, eh? You bet. This wasn't like I was paranoid, thinking management were monitoring me, just more like there was someone hiding somewhere watching me. I suppose on days there is so much going on with all the patients milling around, I was so busy I didn't have the time to think about anything else. On nights the patients are all in their beds, the corridors are dimly lit, with everywhere quiet, I just wasn't used to it. At first I did smile at my own reaction because this was why I wanted to get onto nights, for an easy life and minimal contact with people, so I figured I would get used to it in time.

Anyway, I was right about one thing, there wasn't much to do on nights so maybe that accounted for my unease, you know having too much time to think makes you imagine crazy stuff – hell after all I did work in a mad house!

The first night was creepy enough and nowhere close to how it got. I put it down to having to walk around the hospital during the night. These corridors are very long with too many places that don't catch the light, causing shadows. I found myself shivering and yes, I did start to imagine I saw things that really weren't there until I got closer to them. There was one particular place, walking past the chapel, was guaranteed to give me the creeps during the night patrol and not only because the light was dimmer there either. I felt an atmosphere I couldn't have described to anyone even if I wanted to discuss it.

Sometimes I caught the odd scrapping sound from somewhere inside the chapel. There was no way I was going in there to find out if one of the patients was out of their bed. I got to walking very briskly past there. I honestly didn't think it would spook me like that. After all, the place was the same one I walked around on the day shifts for years wasn't it?

They call this night time job 'patrol' which was mostly about checking on everything, counting the number of patients occupying beds, that was called 'bed state', although it didn't take account of long stay patients, as they were going nowhere (unless, o'course, one died). No, they needed to know if there were any vacant beds on the acute admission wards, in case of an emergency admission in the night or to supply information for the next day's clinics for any new intake admitted from there. These were those crazy people who needed somewhere safe to go or might be dangerous to people outside. Doing 'bed state' was quite a boring task, but necessary see. Sounds simple enough if everyone is fast asleep occupying their allocated beds and was what I expected. I knew we gave out medication at the end of the day shift to get them ready for a long night's uninterrupted sleep, so counting them on each ward posed no problems if they were where they should have been.

I was surprised on my second night though. This time I was more prepared for a long boring shift by bringing something with me to read. I was sitting at the desk in the office doing just that, I'd left the door open so I could hear any of the buzzers go off or just any noise at all if one of the patients got out of bed. I was particularly engrossed in my newspaper reading about yet another disaster somewhere in the world, when my attention was drawn to a sudden movement out in the corridor through the open door. I figured one of the patients must be visiting the loo, since no one came to bother me, I ignored it. When it happened again I got up to check. I wasn't sure, thinking 'did I see something?' like one of those moments on days when I thought I glimpsed a movement around a corner, though nothing specific I was able to describe. Other than that there was nothing to see.

There was a slight scraping sound drew my attention the third time, only this time one of the patients stood at the end of the ward corridor just looking at me. This one I figured must be a new admission because I hadn't seen her before when I worked days. She looked very young to be on an adult ward, that much I could tell even though, as I said, the lighting was quite poor at night.

She certainly looked extremely sad. She was quite an oddity because she was wearing a long white cotton nightdress to her ankles. The patients usually wore fleecy pyjamas or onesies because it was really cold in here at night when they tried to save on heating. This was strange in itself without adding the fact she appeared so pale she looked all one colour – white. Even her skin, what I could see of it. She looked so painfully thin and frail I thought she might fall over if you blew on her. She stared at me for a moment longer before she turned to walk away neither in the direction of the toilets nor the patient's rooms.

My shout of "Hey!" didn't distract her as she made no reply. I followed after her but couldn't see where she went, so I went to check on each of my patients to find out which room she came from to see if I could identify who she was from the white board in the office where we wrote the current list of patient's names in room numbered squares. Needless to say I couldn't find any of the patients missing or any new names on the board in the office. At the time I wrote her off as someone straying onto my ward from one of the other wards and ended up falling asleep slumped over the desk, so if she came back I would have missed her.

I can't say I was too disappointed at first with the night shift, after all I imagined it was quiet with not much going on. I was right as far as the patients were concerned because they rarely gave me any trouble. This was certainly nothing like during the ward 'community therapy' meetings where they often attacked each other verbally or even physically. Mostly they were as good as gold being fast asleep on night shifts.

The young girl who visited during the night I couldn't find on any of the nearby ward registers or identify her after making enquiries. One night I woke up suddenly from one of my naps, having fallen asleep again head down on the desk, I found myself being watched by another male nurse. He gave me quite a start at first followed by a flush of guilt because I was caught out sleeping. My immediate thought being I was failing in my duty, he would report me and I would get into trouble, so I made out I'd just closed my eyes for a second whilst I was doing my reports. I always kept them on the desk y'see in case I needed to pretend I was actually working.

He looked a bit fierce, scowling like he was disapproving of me, before he walked off saying nothing. I only made a few enquiries to try to find out where he worked because I didn't want to let on and draw attention to me sleeping on duty. When it happened again I did notice he was wearing a different uniform, nothing like our tunics which were blue; he wore a white outfit, I did think was strange as I thought we all wore the same kind of uniforms. Then I remembered the description of the apparition Janice the receptionist claimed she saw one night whilst working late which she said she'd seen in some old photos from the past.

I couldn't get it out of my head. You can see how my doubts began to change my way of thinking? Afterwards it seemed quite normal to see the young girl or even the male nurse, which was a big leap from not believing in that sort of thing to having to accept these appearances weren't actually real.

6

I never did have any real bother with the patients whilst working nights, but I can't say that about the things I had absolutely no control over. I was reminded of the incident of the office mirror when someone from the semi-secure unit on the next floor down asked me about the noises during the night on my ward. One night I heard a lot of commotion coming from the patient's day room, this being empty at night, was where the patients spent most of their time during the day, also where the 'community treatment' meetings were held.

The room was large containing some more informal furniture, like armchairs and couches, as well as tables and chairs where the patients ate their meals communally, although some of them do prefer to take their food to eat in the privacy of their own rooms which we try to discourage for lots of reasons. One of the main reasons is to monitor the patient's food intake. Some can get a bit anorexic whilst in hospital on drugs and I'll say nothing about the quality of the food which a lot of patients find unpalatable. There was always a member of staff around to observe them in the day room.

Mostly eating together is part of the idea of Community which for me was something I tried hard to avoid as much as possible. I could see some patients were uncomfortable having to eat their meals with so many strangers. Sometimes the odd spat would break out because one of the more disturbed patients would try to steal something off the plate of another, making you have to intervene.

Anyway, this particular night there is an absolute kafuffle coming from the day room which has me running down the corridor with a view to breaking up a fight, or so I thought. I also didn't want the noise to wake up the other patients. For me, experiencing the day shift taught me to respond quickly. In those days I was fit and could easily react immediately. I'm saying this because I took no time at all to get along to the day room.

When I pushed open the door, the noise stopped and there was no one there. Apart from a lot of toppled chairs there was only a spider plant looking like it fell off one of the window sills, otherwise the room looked like normal and there was absolute silence. What I'd heard was very loud and unruly, so I expected a number of patients to be involved. I went to check all the patients on the ward to find them all sound asleep snoring noisily in their beds. I tidied the place as best I could leaving only a bit of compost scattered around for Joyce to clear up next day having stuffed most of the compost back into the pot with the sorry looking plant. To get the vacuum cleaner out Joyce used might have woken the patients up so didn't want to risk it.

When I finally got back to the office I have to admit I could find no explanation for either the noise or the mess I found in the day room. No amount of telling myself one of the patients was responsible, that they could have caused the noise as well as the mess then managed to slip back into bed to pretend to be asleep, could I believe. There just wasn't the time to do that. Like I say I was pretty fit in those days and my reaction was immediate. My doubts began to emerge.

What made me finally admit fully about the 'presences' in the night was when I bump into one of the other hospital night shift staff one day when I'm on my 'nights off'. I was in a café in town having a bite to eat. I did once in a while back then because I missed using the canteen for some of my meals as it wasn't open at night. Living on your own, you always eat alone, and it gets a bit, well let's just say you crave peripheral noise, not so much someone to talk to, as I have said I always hated that, although being on nights changed me a lot. I suppose it was not speaking to anyone at all or more likely *hearing* someone speak to me. I know I'm a loner and don't like too much 'people' noise. That was from growing up with a lot of continual rowing when my parents shouted at each other.

Anyway, this chap Barnie I recognised, worked nights on another ward, where I saw him occasionally when I did the bed state. I noticed him, not because he is black like me, more because he has huge frightened eyes which in a black face, are emphasised even more making him look permanently frightened. He brought his cuppa over and slid down on the chair opposite me launching immediately into the same stuff I used to get on days. No, not the personal tales of woe, but the things he's seen on nights. He seemed surprised I'm not showing the same alarm, he couldn't believe I hadn't seen things. Actually, I didn't let on in case I might prolong the conversation or even encourage some kind of loose friendship to develop.

The point of telling this is I've discovered most night staff also slipped themselves a sleeping pill and found a vacant bed for a nap to pass the night quicker. It was, he said, the only way to avoid some of the worst disruptive activity that happens during the night. I was tempted to ask for an example just to see if any of his stories were the same as mine. I did also wonder what happened if there was a genuine emergency situation with one of his patients, but to ask him would have prolonged the encounter.

He did tell me back in the day patients weren't always treated very well and how they were the worst of times Echo Heights has seen. I had no doubt about him being serious, he looked a troubled man. He also tells me, although he seems very reluctant, my job vacancy arose because the person in the job before me killed themselves. He looked terrified when he added, "*He hung himself at work!*" I must admit that bit did bother me. I confess when the activity got a bit too much on my ward I did take his advice popping a sleeping pill to get through the shift.

I'm not sure whether this conversation specifically raised my interest in what happened years ago, or whether I was coming round to it anyway, I did begin to look into the history of the Asylum. I already found the old style ledgers piled at the back of the patients records section, you know, the spill over room where the toilets are. In those days they used these massive leather bound tomes you could barely pick up they were enormous. Even in those days they used to take a picture of the patient when they were admitted, mostly a head and shoulders black and white or sepia image. I imagined they used the old tripod cameras with plates I've seen in books. A patient could be an inmate for most of their lives especially if you take account of the ones who were born feeble minded, it was probably all their lives.

What passed for patient notes then was like I said a one line entry once a year, signed by the senior physician. I reckon they were more of a note to show they were still alive like a census as there was no attempt made to assess their actual mental state or whether it improved or deteriorated; 'works well in the garden' doesn't even come close does it?

Later when experimental 'treatments' were introduced they did start to record more about the patients, mostly about how they took to 'treatments' like hot and cold water baths, bloodletting and purgatives, the use of restraints, and the more barbaric ones like boring holes into the skull thought to relieve pressure. Mostly from what I can tell looking at old patient notes Echo Heights was used to keep 'inmates' in custody and I reckon was not much different to being in prison, was it?

The saddest ones for me were the young girls who were admitted to Echo Heights because they were pregnant so were considered to be defective for getting themselves into the family way. What I read was always written as if it was their fault. There was enough evidence around to know a lot of them were raped, often by a member of their own family who put them away in the Asylum to save their own reputations. Sometimes even their babies were given to a neighbour who happened to be childless although there's no record of that.

I found out later from looking through the old records the girl I saw my first time on nights was one of them. She was fourteen when she got admitted. Her name was Elizabeth, known always as Lizzie. She would have been one of the lifers who eventually got put in an old folk's home when they shut down most of the old long stay mental hospitals, only Lizzie died giving birth to her baby in Echo Heights which was why I suppose she always looked so sad. The baby was recorded as a boy. From what I could see she never got to hold him before they took him away and there's no record of what happened to him afterwards. I have it in my head the times I saw her – maybe I didn't say, it was a regular occurrence – she was searching the asylum looking for her baby which was why she looked so sad.

Anyway, wasn't long after my chance meeting with Barnie, plans were put in place to close the Asylum. Patients were transferred to the new psychiatric unit at the teaching hospital whilst the long stay went to a variety of community facilities. I worked at the new unit for a while after until I retired but it just wasn't the same, I kind of missed the old place. I realised Echo Heights was more like a 'place of safety' giving asylum if you like, certainly than a hospital ward like other medical facilities. Echo Heights was self-contained then with its own grounds, even if it was old and depressing to look at.

The new unit was on the ground floor of a modern teaching hospital, so at least they gave some thought where to put it. We used to have a few problems at Echo Heights with patients trying to jump out of the windows being on the third floor up especially after they got rid of the old sash windows which didn't open far enough to allow it.

Mind you the new unit didn't stop patients trying to kill themselves because they could wander off the wards. We did have one who went over to the multi-story car park opposite to do just that. What made things worse was the patient was one of our own nurses who got admitted. There's an irony somewhere in that and made me think about retiring, getting out while I still felt sane.

What happened to Echo Heights?

They sold it off including the huge expanse of grounds where they built a whole estate of small houses. As to the actual Asylum building, this was converted into luxury flats with a complex of all sorts of facilities, like a laundry, indoor swimming pool and a gym. Who would have thought you could change the old depressing building into something people wanted to buy to live in. How do I know? I bought one of them. In fact, I was one of the first to get one so I got the pick of the first phase when they planned it.

I took the one closest to where I used to work when I was on the acute admissions ward. They did a good job. It's very modern and tastefully done. As I was one of the first in I was lucky to be asked by the agents to be their site representative – well it's more of a caretaking role really. I do a few jobs around the complex like showing any prospective buyers around when there's a vacancy. I earn a bit of pocket money, not that I need it really because over the years I've put a bit by for a rainy day, well I led a simple life so it soon mounts up.

The thing I do mostly is to ensure we get the right peoplc in here, not you understand I have much to do with them if I can help it, I don't encourage them in case I get to hear all their problems. I like a quiet life. Occasionally I bump into someone I know from the past who asks me what it's like living here or if they're really straight with you they ask why I wanted to come here, as not many of them would have especially if they knew about what used to happen here on the nightshift.

I've even been asked directly if it still happens. I don't say much though; it's none of their business is it? What happens here stays here and anything out of the ordinary, well that's just for me to know. Mostly these days if I can't sleep I pop a pill to help me get some sleep because it does seem like as you get older you need less sleep and it can be a long drawn out business now I'm here on the day shift as well as the night shift.

    I will say one thing though, I never get lonely. I see a lot of folk I recognise and a few I used to know like Lizzie, she's still searching for her baby I reckon. I don't bother them and they don't bother me. Why don't I ask them to leave? Well where would they go? After all, seems to me they have more right to be here than I do. It's them who let me stay and mostly they're no trouble, after all, the place was an asylum – somewhere to offer protection and safety to all of us.

THE END

We'd like to know if you enjoyed the book. Please consider leaving a review on the platform from which you purchased the book

Milton Keynes UK
Ingram Content Group UK Ltd.
UKHW010626150124
436059UK00001B/189